Dilly Dog's Dizzy Dancing

by Barbara deRubertis • illustrated by R.W. Alley

THE KANE PRESS / NEW YORK

Alpha Betty's Class

STAR of the BOOK

Alexander Anteater

Bobby Baboon

Corky Cub

Dilly Dog

Eddie Elephant

Frances Frog

Gertie Gorilla

Hanna Hippo

Lana Llama

Izzy Impala

Jeremy Jackrabbit

Kylie Kangaroo

Maxwell Moose

Nina Nandu

Oliver Otter

Polly Porcupine

Quentin Quokka

Rosie Raccoon

Sammy Skunk

Tessa Tiger

Umma Ungka

Victor Vicuna

Walter Warthog

Xavier Ox

Yoko Yak

Zachary Zebra

Alpha Betty

Library of Congress Cataloging-in-Publication Data

deRubertis, Barbara.
Dilly Dog's dizzy dancing / by Barbara deRubertis ; illustrated by R.W. Alley.
p. cm. — (Animal Antics A to Z)
Summary: Teacher Alpha Betty demonstrates new ways of dancing to Dilly Dog so that
Dilly can continue to dance without creating mishaps.
ISBN 978-1-57565-307-5 (lib. bdg. : alk. paper) — ISBN 978-1-57565-303-7 (pbk. : alk. paper)
[1. Dogs—Fiction. 2. Dance—Fiction. 3. Animals—Fiction. 4. Alphabet—Fiction. 5.
Humorous stories.] I. Alley, R. W. (Robert W.), ill. II. Title.
PZ7.D4475Dl 2010
[E]—dc22   2009024485

10 9 8 7 6 5 4 3 2 1

First published in the United States of America in 2010 by Kane Press, Inc.
Printed in Hong Kong
Reinforced Library Binding by Muscle Bound Bindery, Minneapolis, MN

Series Editor: Juliana Hanford
Book Design: Edward Miller

Animal Antics A to Z is a trademark of Kane Press, Inc.

www.kanepress.com

Dilly was a dancing dog.
She loved doing her dizzy dances.

Some of her dancing was very daring.
And some was downright dangerous!

Dilly Dog's dizzy dancing led to
disaster after disaster.

The kids at Alpha Betty's school thought
Dilly was a little daffy.

They worried about Dilly!

7

At dawn one day, Dilly was doing her usual dizzy dancing.

She bounced on her bed as she did a wild dance.

Suddenly she hit the ceiling. BANG!

Then she hit the floor. THUD!

"DILLY!" called Daddy Dog.

"Come downstairs and see what you've done!"

9

Dilly Dog felt dreadful when she
saw the disaster.

A flower pot was damaged.
Daffodils were dumped on the floor.

"I'm sorry, Daddy," said Dilly with dismay.
"My dancing was a little too dizzy."

"Oh, Dilly," Daddy replied.
"I know you adore your dizzy dancing.
But do TRY to be a bit more careful!"

The next day after school, Dilly danced down to the boat dock.

"She's a darling dog," whispered Dory Duck, who worked at the dock.

"But she's a tad dippy."

"She's definitely a dear," whispered Dory's helper, Danny.

"But she's a tad dotty."

Suddenly, Dilly decided to dance ON
the boat dock.

She was NOT wearing a life jacket.
And Dilly was dizzy from dancing.

She darted. She dipped.
She dove through the air.

"Be careful!" cried Dory and Danny together.

But Dilly Dog accidentally danced
right off the end of the dock.

The water was deep.
Dilly was in danger!

Without delay, Dory and Danny dove down into the deep, dark water.

They dragged Dilly up, up, up.

Dilly dog-paddled back to the dock.

Dory and Danny duck-paddled beside her.

Daddy Dog came dashing down to the dock.

"Dilly! You're drenched!" said Daddy.
"And you could have drowned!"

"I'm sorry, Daddy," said Dilly with dismay.
"My dancing was definitely too dizzy."

"Dilly," said Daddy. "It makes me sad.
But I must ask you to stop dancing."

Then he bundled her up
and carried her home.

Dilly Dog was feeling dreadful when
she arrived at school the next day.

She told Alpha Betty about the
disaster on the bed.

She told Alpha Betty about the
disaster on the dock.

Dilly hung her head and cried.

"Daddy is disappointed in me.
My friends think I'm dopey.
I'm really down in the dumps."

Dilly's tears dripped on her dress.

"Don't be sad, Dilly!" said Alpha Betty.

"You are a dear little dog. You just need to learn to dance *differently*."

Then Alpha Betty said something
that dumbfounded Dilly Dog.

"Did you know that I used to be
a dancer?" Alpha Betty asked.

"No!" whispered Dilly.

"Yes!" said Alpha Betty.

"I can show you **delightful** dances!
Dreamy dances! DAZZLING dances!
Would you like to learn?"

"Oh, YES!" whispered Dilly.

Alpha Betty did some dance steps.

Dilly tried to do them, too.

Some of the steps were difficult.

Some were demanding.

But Dilly was determined.

Dilly Dog danced home that day.

But she danced differently than
she had ever danced before.

She waved to Dory and Danny Duck.

They called, "Hello, Dilly!
You're doing a dandy dance today!"

"Daddy! Look!" said Dilly
when she arrived home.

"I'm done with dizzy dancing!
Watch me dance NOW!"

Daddy was delighted with Dilly's new dance!

"Dilly!" he cried. "Your dance is *dazzling*!"

Her smile was dazzling, too.

And Dilly never had a dancing disaster again.

(Well, almost never!)

STAR OF THE BOOK: THE DOG

FUN FACTS

- Home: All over the world! Dogs are the oldest known animal pets.
- Family: There are more than 150 breeds of dogs, and they are in the same family as wolves and foxes. There are also millions of lovable mutts, like Dilly, who are a mixture of breeds!
- Size: Dogs come in every size and shape, from the tiny Chihuahua to the huge Great Dane.
- Favorite foods: Mostly meats and grains. And doggie biscuits!
- **Did You Know?** Dogs have amazing hearing and an awesome sense of smell—much better than humans!

LOOK BACK

Learning to identify letter sounds (phonemes) at the beginning, middle, and end of words is called "phonemic awareness."

- The word *dog* <u>begins</u> with the *d* sound. Listen to the words on page 30 being read again. When you hear a word that <u>begins</u> with the *d* sound, bark like a dog!
- The word *sad* <u>ends</u> with the *d* sound. Listen to the words on page 24 being read again. When you hear a word that <u>ends</u> with the *d* sound, quack like a duck!
- **Challenge**: The word *middle* has the *d* sound in the <u>middle</u>! Listen to the words on page 10 being read again. There is ONE word that <u>begins</u> with the *d* sound AND has the *d* sound in the <u>middle</u>. What is the word?

TRY THIS!

Dilly's Dizzy Dancing Game
Listen carefully as each word in the word bank is read aloud.

- If the word <u>begins</u> with the *d* sound, jump in the air!
- If the word <u>ends</u> with the *d* sound, sit down!
- If the word <u>begins</u> and <u>ends</u> with the *d* sound, spin around once!

dizzy bed dance
darted dock held
dress sad dear
delighted

FOR MORE ACTIVITIES, go to Dilly Dog's website: www.kanepress.com/AnimalAntics/DillyDog
You'll also find a recipe for Dilly Dog's Dilly Dip for Vegetables!